STAR TREK™
TREK THE HALLS

Written by
Robb Pearlman

LITTLE, BROWN AND COMPANY
New York Boston

Illustrated by
Luke Flowers

Cover illustration by Luke Flowers. Cover design by Carolyn Bull.

Little, Brown and Company
Hachette Book Group
1290 Avenue of the Americas
New York, NY 10104
Visit us at LBYR.com
startrek.com

First Edition: October 2022

Little, Brown and Company is a division of Hachette Book Group, Inc.
The Little, Brown name and logo are trademarks of Hachette Book Group, Inc.

The publisher is not responsible for websites (or their content) that are not
owned by the publisher.

Library of Congress Cataloging-in-Publication Data
Names: Pearlman, Robb, author. | Flowers, Luke, illustrator.
Title: Star Trek: trek the halls / Robb Pearlman, Luke Flowers.
Other titles: Trek the halls
Description: First edition. | New York : Little, Brown and Company, 2022. |
Summary: "In a delightfully bright and irreverent twist on "Deck the Halls," this commercial, lighthearted,
and nondenominational holiday picture book features beloved Star Trek characters and locales and is a
festive must-have for Trek fans of all generations!" —Provided by publisher.
Identifiers: LCCN 2021048361 | ISBN 9780316361187 (hardcover) | ISBN 9780316361286 (ebook)
Subjects: LCSH: Star Trek television programs—Juvenile humor. | CYAC: Stories in rhyme.
LCGFT: Stories in rhyme. | Picture books. | Humorous poetry.
Classification: LCC PZ8.3.P2747135 St 2022 | DDC 811/.6—dc23/eng/20211004
LC record available at https://lccn.loc.gov/2021048361

ISBNs: 978-0-316-36118-7 (hardcover), 978-0-316-36128-6 (ebook),
978-0-316-42408-0 (ebook), 978-0-316-42418-9 (ebook)

Printed in the United States
PHX
10 9 8 7 6 5 4 3 2 1

For Erin Macdonald, a gift.
—RP

Thank you to the crew of Memory Alpha for providing an expansive
universe of resources and inspiration. Your celebration of all things
Star Trek has been the "final frontier" for me as I researched and illustrated
this festive tribute. Happy Holidays to all my fellow Trekkies.
—LF

'Twas the night before stardate 2387.12
when, deep in the Beta Quadrant,
Little Gorn intercepted a subspace transmission.

Little Gorn was very excited to discover that it was a special time for cheer and parties and gifts on Earth. Big Gorn let Little Gorn know that, as members of the Gorn species, they would never have goodwill toward humans or their allies in the United Federation of Planets.

Big Gorn sat down with Little Gorn and told him about some other transmissions he had intercepted about these horrible festivities. . . .

Trek the halls with Bones and Scotty,
Captain Kirk and Spock—Uhura, too.
'Tis the season to go boldly:
Sulu, Chekov, Chapel, and Rand, too.
Don they now brocade apparel,
Amanda and Sarek are now on board,
showing ancient Vulcan greetings.
Family drama cannot be ignored!

Fast away the old year passes—
back now to the 80s for the whales.
Hail the crew, "Ye lads and lasses!"
Scotty cries before the engine fails.

Laughing, quaffing all together,
remembering what they learned on the streets!
Heedless of the wind and weather,
save the animals and gift receipts!

Wesley cites anomalies.
Geordi works inside a Jefferies tube.
If they switch polarities,
they may overtake the looming Cube.

Must resist assimilation—
that is what Jean-Luc wants them to do.
Lights on trees are so much nicer
than implants glowing over you!

See the crew meet in Ten Forward,
raising glasses to the holiday,
drinking grapes from Picard's château.
Guinan saved them for a special day.
Worf drinks bloodwine, Data nothing.
Troi counsels Reg, "Don't be afraid."
Will pulls out the seat beside her—
why's he always sitting down that way?

Holidays are for gift-giving,
Quark wants them all to so believe.
He sells gift cards for his living—
good till closing time on Friday eve!

Odo's not sure; he checks his notes.
Jake and Nog think that they'll be just fine
regifting self-sealing stem bolts:
It's the thought that counts on DS9!

Holosuites are great for parties.
"Ev'rybody, let's have fun," says Dax.
Julian is such a smarty,
thwarting the Dominion's space attacks.

Garak has the best apparel—
custom-made tuxes just look so chill.
To celebrate, he'll sing a carol,
of universal peace, joy, and goodwill!

"There is coffee in that neb'la."
Janeway's on the bridge of Voyager.
Not the decaf—she likes reg'la'.
It's what Tom thought he'd give to her.

Following the course before them,
Starfleet and Maquis go get the stuff.
Work together; do not condemn.
Just forget rivalries—'nough's enough!

See what Neelix lays before us.
Everything we'd want this holiday.
The Doctor is not all that impressed.
He can't taste a thing now anyway.

Harry thinks about his mother.
B'Elanna smiles because she's not tense.
Seven wants more to discover.
She announces, "Fun will now commence!"

Deck E in the NX sickbay—
Phlox takes care of ev'ryone right there.
Even if you're 'bout to give way,
nobody is too beyond repair.

Growing clones or just a headache,
he'll fix the crew both night and day!
Does he rest or take a break?
You can count on him in every way!

Smear the gel on Trip and Hoshi,
Archer, Malcolm, and Mayweather, too.
T'Pol was left in charge, and so she
watches them celebrate the yule.

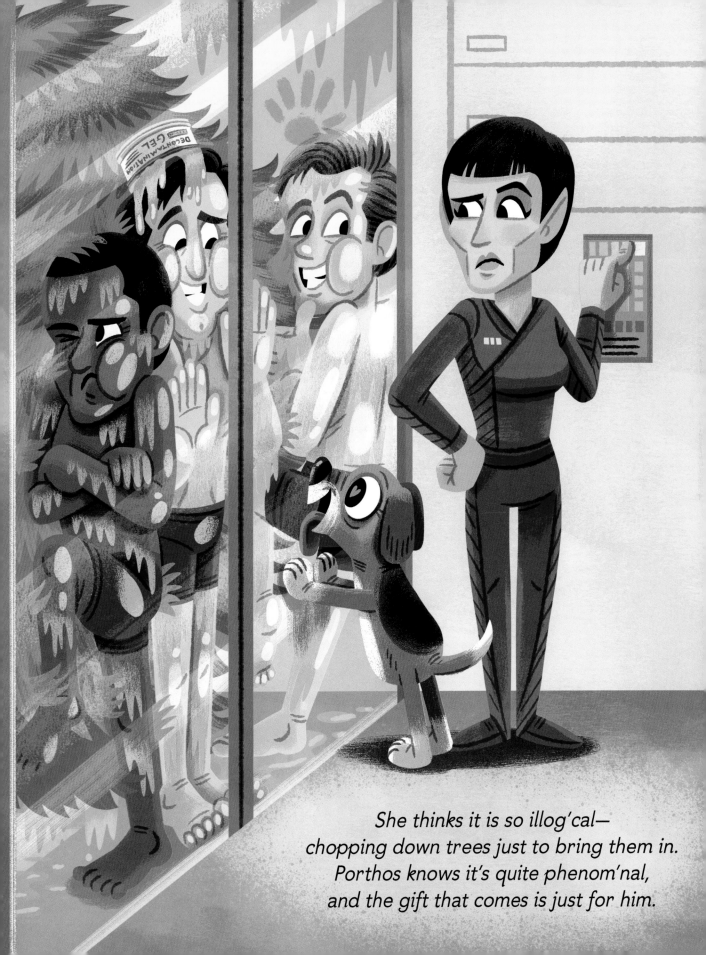

She thinks it is so illog'cal—
chopping down trees just to bring them in.
Porthos knows it's quite phenom'nal,
and the gift that comes is just for him.

Running in the halls with Tilly,
Michael knows just what they have to do.
Holidays are never silly:
Christmas, Hanukkah, and Kwanzaa, too.

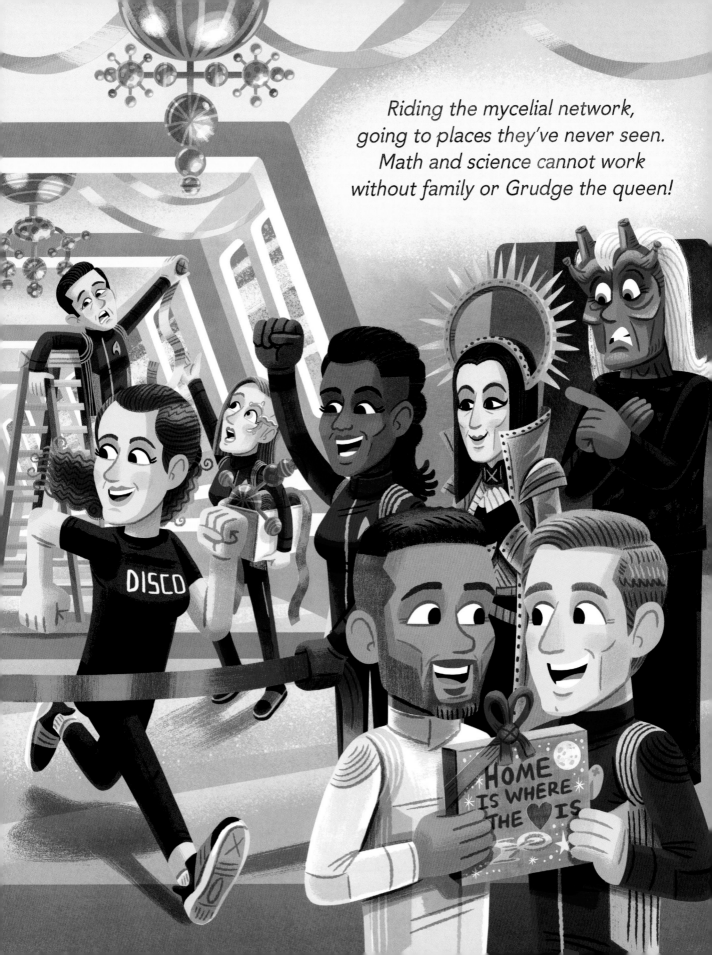

Riding the mycelial network,
going to places they've never seen.
Math and science cannot work
without family or Grudge the queen!

See Starfleet's phasers before us?
They're all set to stun, so don't worry.
Joined together as a chorus,
we are the Gorn Hegemony!

After Big Gorn finished his tales, Little Gorn's blood ran even colder than usual. He now understood how awful Federation "holidays" truly were. He no longer wanted anything to do with the Federation.

As he drifted off to sleep, with visions of insufferable Starfleet captains in his little green head, he heard Big Gorn exclaim . . .